UNICORN ACADEMY
...Where magic happens!

Matilda and Pearl

JULIE SYKES

illustrated by
LUCY TRUMAN

nosy crow

For the very magical
Philippa and Polly

First published in the UK in 2019 by Nosy Crow Ltd
The Crow's Nest, 14 Baden Place, Crosby Row
London, SE1 1YW, UK

Nosy Crow and associated logos are trademarks and/or registered
trademarks of Nosy Crow Ltd

Text copyright © Julie Sykes and Linda Chapman, 2019
Illustrations copyright © Lucy Truman, 2019

The right of Julie Sykes, Linda Chapman and Lucy Truman to be
identified as the authors and illustrator respectively of this work
has been asserted by them in accordance with the Copyright,
Designs and Patents Act 1988.

Printed and bound in the UK by Clays Ltd, Elcograf S.p.A.

Papers used by Nosy Crow are made from wood grown in
sustainable forests.

ISBN: 978 1 78800 463 3

www.nosycrow.com

Matilda followed Pearl's gaze and inhaled sharply. A figure cloaked in black was cantering towards the clearing on a golden-maned unicorn. Matilda vaulted onto Pearl's back but it was too late for them to escape. She gripped Pearl's mane. "What are we going to do now?" she whispered.

UNICORN ACADEMY
...Where magic happens!

HAVE YOU READ?

Sophia and Rainbow

Ava and Star

Isabel and Cloud

Layla and Dancer

Olivia and Snowflake

Rosa and Crystal

Ariana and Whisper

★ ★ ★

LOOK OUT FOR:

Freya and Honey

Violet and Twinkle

Isla and Buttercup

CHAPTER ONE

"Pearl, you moved!" Matilda was trying to draw Pearl, her unicorn, but it wasn't going too well. "Your leg is all wrong in my picture now. Pleeeease stand still."

"Sorry Matilda. I just can't stop thinking about magic. When do you think I'll get mine and what do you think it will be?" Pearl tossed her pink and yellow mane.

"I don't know," said Matilda, re-sketching Pearl's leg.

Pearl began to pirouette in circles. "Maybe I'll be able to make a snow twister, like Crystal!" She

spun faster until she almost tripped over her hooves. Slowing down, she tilted her head and affected a dreamy look. "Or I might get soothing magic like Whisper. Or what about freezing magic?" Pearl held the pose like a statue until finally she wobbled. "Nah. Freezing magic is boring! I wouldn't mind getting wind magic, though, like Golden Briar. Wouldn't it be fun to have wind magic, Matilda?" Pearl blew out through her nostrils with a loud trumpeting sound. She crossed her eyes and blew so hard it made her cheeks wobble. "Or flying magic! Imagine if I had wings!" She leapt into the air with her hooves pointed.

"Pearl! Stop goofing around so I can finish this picture!" Matilda tried to look stern but Pearl looked so funny she started to giggle. Her pencil skittered across her sketchbook as she tried to capture the dancing unicorn.

Pearl began prancing around the field, tapping

flowers with a hoof then making a popping, crackling noise. "Guess what magic now, Matilda?"

"Fire magic," said Matilda.

"And now?" Pearl walked very slowly, lifting each hoof in an exaggerated tiptoe.

"Stop!" Matilda chuckled and dropped her pencil. "How can I draw anything when you keep making me laugh? What sort of magic is that supposed to be? Whatever it is, I hope you don't get it. You look like a circus pony!"

Pearl trotted over and leaned over Matilda's shoulder, nuzzling her dark-red hair. "I don't mind what magic I have. I just wish I could find it," she said, blinking her long eyelashes. "It's summer already. We're halfway through our time at Unicorn Academy. What if I don't find out before the graduation ball in December? And we haven't bonded, either."

All the unicorns at Unicorn Academy were trying to discover their magic power and bond with their rider. When a rider and unicorn bonded, a strand of the rider's hair turned the same colour as their unicorn's mane. Matilda couldn't wait for a pink and yellow streak to appear in her long, red hair. She was sure it would soon. She and Pearl had been best friends ever since their first day at

Matilda and Pearl

the academy when Ms Nettles, the headteacher, had paired them up. At first, Ms Nettles had seemed a little uncertain about it.

"I hope you're not going to be a bad influence on each other," she'd said, frowning behind her glasses. "Since you're both quite disorganised, maybe I should put you with someone else?"

Matilda remembered how she'd crossed her fingers tightly behind her back, hoping that Ms Nettles would let her and Pearl go together. She'd loved Pearl from first sight. Pearl's dark eyes seemed to twinkle with mischief and she was perfect for drawing, too. Her beautiful white coat was patterned with colourful and interesting shapes.

"Do you think Ms Nettles was right? Are we a bad influence on each other?" asked Matilda, straightening her glasses on her nose and remembering the headteacher's words. Maybe

that was why they hadn't found Pearl's magic and bonded.

"Definitely not!" Pearl declared. "We're perfect for each other!" She shook her head. "Just imagine if I'd been paired with Ariana. Nightmare!"

Matilda giggled. "Ariana's not that bad. She's just a lot more organised than us. I've been getting on much better with her since our adventure in the woods."

"That was fun, wasn't it? I loved playing in the river and solving the mystery…" Pearl bucked across the meadow as she remembered.

"Whoa! Pearl, steady on," Ariana called out as she came running across the grass towards them. "You're going to kick someone if you do that. Matilda! Did you forget that Ms Nettles wants to talk to us about the camping trip and scavenger hunt?"

Matilda caught her breath. "I thought the

meeting was tomorrow."

"No, we set off on the trip tomorrow," said Ariana. "You never listen properly. The meeting's starting soon. I've been trying to find you."

"Wait!" Matilda looked at the picture she had been drawing and snorted with laughter. "Look at my picture, Pearl!"

Pearl trotted over. "You've given me wings!" She began to giggle. "I look very strange. Why did you do that?"

Matilda frowned. "I have no idea. I thought I was just drawing what I was seeing."

"I didn't have wings last time I looked," said Pearl looking over her shoulder. "Nope, no wings."

"Come on, Matilda," said Ariana impatiently.

"Diamond dorm will all be in trouble if we arrive late."

"I'll see you later, Matilda," said Pearl. "Come and see me after your meeting." She trotted off towards the stables.

Matilda set off with Ariana but halfway across the field, she stopped. "My pencils and water bottle! Where are they? Did you pick them up for me, Ariana?"

"No, why would I?" asked Ariana.

"I'll have to go back for them," Matilda said, turning around.

Ariana groaned. "Why are you so forgetful?"

Matilda swept her long red hair over her shoulders and hurried back to get her stuff. But after running a few steps she spotted a bright yellow butterfly flitting from flower to flower. She stopped to examine it.

"Matilda!" exclaimed Ariana. "Come on!"

Matilda and Pearl

Matilda sighed and left the butterfly. Ariana needed to chill. So what if they were a bit late? The teachers might tell them off but they wouldn't get into that much trouble. She gathered her possessions into her arms and headed back towards Ariana, the pile teetering unsteadily. "Here, hold this for me." Matilda handed Ariana a water bottle.

Ariana pursed her lips but she took the water bottle and a packet of pencils as it started to slide from Matilda's sketchbook. "You're so disorganised."

Matilda shrugged. Being organised was a lot of hard work and she only liked to work hard at things she enjoyed – like drawing. "So?" she said. "It doesn't matter."

Ariana gave her an exasperated look. "It does! It's good to be organised. Remember our adventure in the woods when the animals turned bad because the waterfall was blocked? We might

not have been able to start the waterfall flowing again if I hadn't been prepared and brought a load of stuff with me."

"I suppose," Matilda conceded.

"Now, we need to get to the meeting and find out how we can prepare for this scavenger hunt and camping trip," said Ariana. She shook her head. "I know it's supposed to be a treat but I'm very surprised the teachers are allowing it. They still don't know who was responsible for the waterfall drying up. You'd think they'd be doing more to try to find out who it was. What if that person strikes again?"

Matilda stared at her. Ariana really did worry about silly things. The teachers were bound to have everything under control. Matilda felt sorry for her anxious friend. She really needed to laugh more. Seeing a beetle on the path ahead of them she suddenly had an idea. She knew exactly how to

get Ariana giggling. She
stopped and pointed
at the beetle.

"Eeek! Watch out!"
she squealed. "It's a
three-headed, snotty-
nose flapdoodle!" She
jumped sideways into
a bed of sparkle lilies,
dragging Ariana with her.

"What? That thing there?" Ariana gasped,
clinging to Matilda's arm. "Is it dangerous?"

Matilda burst out laughing. "Joke!" she exclaimed.
"There's no such thing as a three-headed snotty-
nose flapdoodle. I just made it up! Your face was so
funny, Ariana!"

Ariana glared at her. "Matilda!"

"Girls! Get off those flowers immediately," a
voice shouted. "Whatever do you think you are

doing?"

Ariana jumped off the flowerbed as Ms Bramble, the grumpy head gardener, came stomping up with Ms Willow, the school nurse. "Sorry, Miss!" she gasped as the stout gardener looked at them angrily.

"It was my fault," said Matilda, not wanting to get Ariana in trouble.

"I don't care whose fault it is!" snapped Ms Bramble. "Guardians of the island are supposed to look after all of nature – animals and plants – and you have both just squashed four lilies! Honestly! I've got my hands full with a quiverleaf tree dying without you squashing lilies too!"

"I'm so, so sorry," apologised Ariana.

Matilda felt bad as she looked at the broken lilies. "Yes, me too." She hadn't meant to wreck the flowerbed.

"I'm sure it was just an accident," Ms Willow

said soothingly, tucking a loose strand of hair back into her neat bun. She was young and pretty and her eyes were kind. "You'll be more careful in future, won't you, girls?"

Matilda and Ariana nodded.

Ms Willow smiled at them. "Then we'll say no more about it. Off you run."

Ms Bramble harrumphed and went over to the quiverleaf tree that stood behind the lilies. Matilda noticed that its branches were drooping and its leaves were turning brown. Ms Bramble was carrying a large bucket and a length of green bandage and Ms Willow held a small silver knife. Matilda watched them curiously. Whatever were they doing?

Ariana tugged Matilda by the sleeve. "Come on."

"Coming," said Matilda, her eyes still on the gardener and the school nurse. It was an odd combination of people. What exactly were they going to do with a bucket and a knife?

CHAPTER TWO

Ariana hurried on but Matilda stood, transfixed, as Ms Bramble pressed the point of the knife to the tree and made a small, deep cut in its trunk. A pale liquid oozed out. Ms Willow stepped forward, soaking it up with a wad of cotton. She asked Ms Bramble to hold the cotton against the tree. From her small black medicine bag, she brought out a syringe and a bottle filled with a green liquid. Shaking the bottle, she unscrewed the top and drew the liquid up into the syringe. The liquid was greener than fresh peas and very sparkly. Matilda caught the scent of something sweet and

minty. Ms Willow asked Ms Bramble to remove the wad of cotton from the tree trunk and then she inserted the syringe into the cut. Slowly and carefully, Ms Willow began to inject the sparkly green liquid into the tree.

Matilda couldn't contain her curiosity for a second longer. "What are you doing?"

Ms Bramble swung round. Matilda braced

herself, expecting a long lecture followed by a detention. But Ms Willow broke in before Ms Bramble could speak.

"It's good to see a future guardian of Unicorn Island taking an interest in its wildlife," Ms Willow said with a warm smile. "This quiverleaf tree is dying. I'm hoping that my special herbal remedy will heal it. The medicine has to be infused into the tree. It's a tricky operation. I'm showing Ms Bramble how to do it so that if there's a next time, she can do it herself."

"Is that what's in the syringe? The infusion?" asked Matilda.

"Yes, it is. Once I've finished injecting it then I'll bandage the tree trunk to stop the medicine from leaking back out with the tree's sap. The bandage also protects the tree by preventing germs from entering the cut."

"That's very interesting," said Ariana, who'd

now come back for Matilda. She gave Matilda's arm a tug. "But we really have to go."

"Of course! Off you run," Ms Willows smiled as she flapped her hands, cheerfully shooing them away.

Matilda and Ariana ran all the way to the hall, arriving just as Ms Nettles walked on to the stage. The rest of the school were already in their seats, whispering together. The hall was one of Matilda's favourite places in the school. It had a domed glass roof that was filled with colourful swirls. In the centre of the room was a magical map – a three dimensional model of the island that could transport people anywhere they wanted to go. It was protected by a glimmering force field. At the far end, the grand stage overlooked the room.

"There you are! We thought you were going to miss it," said Rosa, squeezing up next to Violet to make space for them. Freya was at the far end

of the group, her blonde head bent over as she scribbled in her notebook. She loved to invent things and was working on a new idea. She hadn't told the rest of Diamond dorm what it was going to be yet, but she seemed to be spending more and more time lost in her own thoughts.

"Listen carefully, everyone," said Ms Nettles. "This is your first camping trip and there are a lot

of things that you need to know. You'll be going to Dingleberry Dell – a wooded area at the base of the mountains. It's a short ride from the school grounds."

Matilda concentrated very hard for a whole minute before her mind started to wander. It was extremely difficult to pay attention when there were so many things she wanted to draw. Almost without realising it, Matilda's fingers reached for her favourite pencil, which she had skewered in her thick red hair. While Ms Nettles talked about tents, ground mats and sleeping bags, Matilda began to draw the hall in her sketchbook. Her pencil flew across the paper, capturing the grandness of the room and how the domed glass roof filled the space with a soft rainbow light. By her side, Ariana was making notes, nodding to herself and underlining the important points. Finally Ms Nettles finished.

"I wish we could go camping right now. I don't think I can wait until tomorrow," said Rosa as they all left the hall.

"Me neither," Violet agreed. "I hope we're allowed to toast food on the fire. My uncle sent me a bag of chocolate bread. It's even more delicious when it's toasted."

"Yummy," Matilda said, looking up. "I love camping. Food tastes so much nicer when you cook it outdoors."

Ariana frowned. "We'll have to be careful to cook everything thoroughly or we might get sick. And what about the washing up? I think I'll add an extra bucket to my packing list."

"I wish we didn't have to go camping," sighed Freya. "What?" she added, seeing Matilda's incredulous stare. "Imagine this: you're drawing something special and you really want to finish it. Would you want to go camping then? This

thing I'm working on – my invention – I've just reached the exciting bit where I'm ready to start building it. If the camping trip was next week then I wouldn't mind. But this week, I just want to stay behind and build."

"We're only away for one night," said Violet reasonably. "You'll be back before you know it. And no-one will get sick, Ariana."

"Bring your invention with you. I'm going to take my sketchbook," said Matilda

Freya shook her head. "Can't," she said. "It's too big."

"So, if Matilda is busy drawing and Freya is making notes on her invention, does that mean the rest of us get stuck with putting up all the tents?" asked Rosa. "If it does, then watch out you two. We might just put some bugs in your bed."

"And spiders in your slippers," Violet added.

Ariana shuddered. She hated spiders.

"Worms in your wash bag," Rosa giggled. "Beetles in your boots."

"Oooh, yes please. I want bugs, spiders and worms. Don't put beetles in my boots though, in case I accidently squish one." Matilda laughed. She loved a good adventure and nothing was going to put her off the camping trip. Not even the thought of bugs in her bed. It sounded way too exciting! She skipped ahead and ducked behind a statue of a unicorn when no one was looking. Hidden behind the statue, she wrapped her arms round her chest, hugging herself tightly to stop the laughter spilling out as her friends' chattering voices drew closer.

"BOO!" Matilda jumped out, flapping her arms and leaping around. "I'm a vampire bat. I only come out at night. Run before I bite you with my fangs!"

"Aaarrgh!" shrieked Ariana.

"Matilda!" Violet put a hand over her heart. "You scared me!"

"What if there are vampire bats in the dell?" asked Ariana. "Or other dangerous creatures."

"Then we'll chase them away, of course," said Matilda with a shrug.

"Yeah!" said Rosa, high-fiving her. "We're not scared! Diamond dorm is strong and tough. Diamond dorm forever!"

CHAPTER THREE

Matilda was so sleepy she could hardly keep her eyes open. She'd had a busy day and she was looking forward to snuggling down in her bed, but first she had to find her pyjamas. They weren't under her pillow or duvet but there was a pile of clothes on the floor. Matilda prodded it with her toe. Perhaps the pyjamas were in there somewhere? Ariana came over and Matilda got ready for a lecture. Ariana had every reason to be annoyed about the mess as it had spilled on to her side of the room but Ariana was occupied with something else. She handed a piece of

paper to Matilda.

"OK, I've done a list of the things we all need to take on the camping trip. There's one here for each of you," she added, handing them round.

"Thanks, Ariana," the other girls chorused.

"Yeah, thanks," said Matilda, examining the paper. Where had Ariana got it from? It was perfect for drawing on, just the right thickness and with a lovely smooth surface. Matilda's fingers twitched with impatience as she sought for a pencil. She found one tucked behind her ear. Flipping the list over, Matilda began to sketch. First she drew Pearl mid-leap, then as her imagination took hold she gave the unicorn large graceful wings. Then she added a bright blue sky filled with fluffy clouds for Pearl to fly through. *It would be amazing if Pearl had flying magic,* she thought, smiling to herself.

"Matilda!" Ariana exclaimed.

Matilda's pencil skidded across the page.

Guiltily, she looked up. "What?" Why was Ariana looking so cross?

"You've drawn on the list and I bet you haven't even read it!"

"So?" Matilda said, shrugging. "If I forget something it's no big deal, you lot will help me out."

"What if we can't help you? Say you forget something important and no one has a spare?"

The words poured from Ariana. "Why is everything just a huge joke to you? Don't you remember our last trip? What if the person who blocked the waterfall turns up and does more dark magic?"

Violet put a reassuring hand on Ariana's arm. "There hasn't been any trouble since then. You shouldn't worry about it."

Matilda nodded. She didn't like seeing Ariana so unhappy. "Violet's right. The teachers wouldn't be letting us go if there was any danger. You stress too much, Ariana."

Ariana bit her lip and sat down on her bed.

Rosa started to brush her long, dark hair. "Wouldn't it be brilliant if we could work out who it was? Ms Nettles and the other teachers would be so thrilled!"

"But how can we possibly work it out when the teachers haven't?" said Freya, glancing up from

her notepad. "It's not going to happen, Rosa."

"Who knows? Maybe we will find something to help us solve the mystery while we're out camping," said Rosa.

"Ooh yes," said Matilda, her eyes gleaming at the thought.

"No," said Violet firmly, glancing at Ariana's alarmed face. "This is just going to be a fun little camping trip. There'll be no mysteries, no adventures and absolutely no danger."

Matilda caught Rosa's eye and immediately knew what she was thinking – mysteries, adventures and danger sounded like fun!

The following morning, Matilda was the last to leave the dorm room. She hurried after her friends, who had set off to prepare their unicorns long before her. She'd packed her rucksack in a hurry, shoving everything in, and now something

hard was sticking into her back. *I should probably repack it when I get to the stables,* thought Matilda, but when she got there she had so much fun brushing and chatting to Pearl that she forgot.

"So, tell me about this camping trip." Pearl nudged Matilda, then blew in her hair to make her giggle.

"Well," said Matilda, trying to remember what Ms Nettles had said. "Once we get to the dell we're supposed to find somewhere good to make a camp. There's also a scavenger hunt with a prize for the winning team."

"I hope Diamond dorm win the scavenger hunt!" said Pearl eagerly.

"Me too," said Matilda, going to the stable door to fetch Pearl's breakfast. "I bet we have a good chance of winning."

"Huh! In your dreams!" said snooty Valentina, who was coming out of her unicorn's stable.

"Ruby dorm have already found half the things on the list. You'll never beat us!"

"But that's cheating!" protested Matilda. "We're supposed to find the things in the dell. You're not allowed to start the scavenger hunt until we get there."

Valentina smiled smugly. "Whatever."

Matilda glared at her. Horrid Valentina. She looked like a frog with her big bulgy eyes and wide smile. Matilda could feel a picture coming on. She whipped a pencil and her mini sketchbook from her jodhpur pocket. She drew Valentina standing with her arms crossed and a very haughty expression on her face, unaware that a frog

was sitting on her head.

Valentina walked up and looked over her shoulder.

"Really, Matilda," she said, looking at it down her long nose. "Is that your best work? Who's it supposed to be, then? You can't draw and you're going to lose the scavenger hunt for Diamond dorm. Look at you. You've lost half your camping stuff already!" Valentina pointed at Matilda's rucksack. She had put it on the floor by the stable door and it had fallen over, spilling the contents. "I feel sorry for the rest of Diamond dorm. I'm very glad you're not on my team!"

Her words stung and Matilda flushed. "I wouldn't want to be on your team anyway," she retorted.

Valentina smiled meanly. "You know, I really don't know how your dorm put up with you. I bet they wish they had someone else instead." She

saw Matilda's red face. "Aw, have I upset the ickle baby?"

"No. I was just thinking how lucky your dorm are," said Matilda. Valentina blinked in surprise. Matilda's hand flew across the page, altering her drawing, giving Valentina the head of a big frog. "Because if we have to collect a tree frog in the scavenger hunt, your team will have one already!" she said, holding the picture up.

Rosa emerged from Crystal's stable. She shrieked with laughter when she saw the drawing.

Valentina scowled. "You're a loser, Matilda! And we'll see who's laughing at the end of the day!" She stormed away.

Rosa giggled. "Oh dear, I think you upset her. What a pity!" Her eyes sparkled.

Matilda went to Pearl's stable and shoved everything back into her rucksack.

"Are you OK?" Pearl asked. Matilda abandoned

her packing and turned and hugged her. Pearl nuzzled Matilda's hair. "Your eyes are all glittery."

Matilda bit her lip. She was more upset by Valentina's words than she wanted to admit, but she knew she could tell Pearl anything. "You don't think she's right, do you, Pearl?" she whispered.

"That the others are wishing I wasn't on their team?"

"Absolutely not!" Pearl blew on her cheek. "Don't listen to Valentina. She's just being mean."

"I do try not to listen when Valentina's unkind." Matilda managed a small smile as she stroked Pearl's soft face. Once mean words were out it was hard to ignore them.

There was the sound of a whistle blowing outside. Rosa popped her head around the stable door. "Come on, Matilda!" she cried excitedly. "Ms Nettles wants to talk to us!"

CHAPTER FOUR

The pupils gathered together in the yard for last minute instructions. Ms Nettles stood on a mounting block with Ms Rivers, the strict Geography and Culture teacher who was going to be accompanying the students. Ms Nettles clapped her hands to get everyone's attention. When the yard was totally silent, she began.

"There are a few important things you must pay attention to before you leave. Firstly, the scavenger hunt competition: the winner is the first team back with everything on the list. That's the whole team. Ms Rivers shall be camping at the

entrance to Dingleberry Dell and her tent is your finishing point."

"Secondly, and more importantly," she continued, "Though I know you're all keen to win the competition, do not put the scavenger hunt ahead of pitching your tent. You must ensure that you are all able to sleep safely tonight! And pick your campsite carefully. Last year, some students pitched their tent on an ant hill." Her lips twitched as she waited for the laughter to fade. "They did not have a comfortable night's sleep! And don't leave putting up your tent until dark. Pitching a tent at night is almost impossible. Finally, no magic can be used in the scavenger hunt." Ms Nettles silenced the groans with a hand. "Many unicorns have still not found their magic. It would not be fair to let those lucky ones who have use it for this task, especially since the prize for winning is something quite special."

Matilda and Pearl

"What is it?" asked Miki from Topaz dorm.

"You'll have to wait and see, Miki." Ms Nettles said mysteriously. "Better still, you'll have to win and see! Now, Ms Rivers will lead the way to the dell. Go and get your unicorns! There's a scavenger hunt to win!"

A loud cheer rang out, sending the bluebirds perched on the fence fluttering up with alarmed squawks.

The sun was shining and it was a lovely ride to the dell. The mountains rose up behind the cluster of trees, tall and craggy, their peaks silhouetted against the sapphire-blue sky. At the entrance to the dell stood a tree that had turned completely white. The other trees clustered in a thick mass behind it, birds singing and squirrels scampering from branch to branch.

"That white tree was once struck by lightning,

children. It's easy to spot, and I shall camp just here," Ms Rivers told the students. "When you have completed the scavenger hunt, come and find me. Now, off you all go!"

Everyone whooped and set off into the trees. At

first there were students and unicorns everywhere but gradually they all separated, following different paths. Rosa led the way for Diamond Dorm. "Let's get far away from everyone else!" she said, heading for the centre of the dell.

They cantered through the trees, their unicorns leaping nimbly over roots and stones on the track. At last, when the noise from the other students had faded and they were completely alone, Rosa and Crystal halted in a grassy clearing. "OK, let's have a look at the list," Rosa said. Each team had been given a list of things they had to find in the dell. Everyone crowded round as Rosa scanned the piece of paper.

"It says we need a green feather, a six-petal daisy, an orange leaf, something pink, a sparkly hag stone – that's a stone with a hole in the middle – and a sprig of red heather," she said. "Should we get started?"

"I think we should sort our camp out first," said Ariana. "Let's put the tents up before it gets dark, like Ms Nettles told us to."

"But it won't be dark for ages," argued Rosa.

"I know. Why don't we find some of the things

on the list and then find somewhere to camp?" suggested Violet.

"But if we want to win the scavenger hunt we should find all the things first," Rosa disagreed.

As they continued to argue about what to do, Matilda pulled out her sketchbook and started to draw the trees around her. It was a very pretty clearing, with a sparkling stream running through it and pink and purple flowers growing around the base of the trees. She was drawing a squirrel when she became aware that Rosa was talking to her.

"Matilda! Did you hear what I just asked? We're taking a vote. Are you in or out?"

"In or out of what?" said Matilda in confusion.

Rosa frowned. "Honestly, Matilda. You never listen, do you? We're voting on whether we should find somewhere to camp or look for the things on the list first."

"Oh." Matilda frowned. "Well, why don't we just camp here and then start looking for the scavenger hunt stuff?"

The others looked round. "I suppose this would be a good place to camp," said Ariana thoughtfully. "It's got a stream for water and it's flat and sheltered."

"And look!" Violet jumped off Twinkle and ran to a clump of round, red-tipped bushes. "Red heather!" she said, pulling a sprig off. "It's one of the things we need. We might find some of the other things right here too! Good idea, Matilda."

"I suppose we could camp here, but we can't spend too long putting up our tents," said Rosa. "I want to win this competition!" She got off Crystal. "Come on, everyone. Be as quick as you can!"

Matilda dismounted and caught sight of a large black-and-white bird perched on a rock

by the stream, watching for fish. Her fingers itched to draw it but she stopped herself. She still remembered Valentina's words and she didn't want to be the reason why Diamond dorm lost the competition.

Everyone got stuck into pitching the tents.

"Now to make it look homely," said Ariana, when the brightly coloured tents were finally up. "Let's unpack our rucksacks and get our sleeping bags out." Her sleeping bag was tied to her rucksack in a neat roll.

Matilda looked at it and then looked at her own rucksack. Her heart sank into her boots.

"Oh no!" she groaned. "I haven't got my sleeping bag. It came untied when I dropped

my rucksack in Pearl's stable. I meant to tie it back on but I forgot."

Ariana put her hands on her hips. "Matilda, this is just not funny. This is why I gave you a list. If you hadn't scribbled all over it, maybe you'd have checked it before we left and remembered your sleeping bag!"

"Honestly Matilda, you're useless. We'll lose the scavenger hunt if we have to go back to the academy for it." Rosa scowled. "You heard what Ms Rosemary said, we all have to finish together."

"I can't believe you've forgotten your sleeping bag!" said Freya. "Now we're going to be stuck here in these woods for even longer. You're so stupid, Matilda!"

Matilda hung her head. She hardly ever cried but now her eyes stung with tears. She hadn't meant to let everyone down.

Violet hurried over to her. "Look, don't worry.

We can go back and get it and if we lose the competition, well, so what? We'll still have fun camping."

Rosa's annoyed exclamation left Matilda in no doubt about what she thought of that. She quickly rubbed her eyes. She didn't want the others to see she was crying.

"It's OK," she said, turning away quickly so they couldn't see. "I'll just sleep on that heather over there."

"But it's not very soft," said Violet in concern.

"I don't mind," said Matilda, carrying her rucksack over to the heather. A sweet smell of burnt sugar wafted towards her. She sniffed in surprise.

"Matilda." Pearl urgently nudged her hand. "Your sleeping bag is over there – look!"

Matilda followed her gaze and saw a dark-purple sleeping bag lying near the heather. Relief

shot through her. She must have brought it with her after all and just dropped it as they entered the clearing!

Matilda jogged towards it but as she drew closer the bag seemed to vanish and change into a dark-purple bush. She pulled up in surprise. What had just happened?

"It's gone!" Pearl was equally confused.

Matilda's brow furrowed. That was the second time she'd seen something that wasn't there. First there were the wings that she'd drawn on Pearl in her picture and now the sleeping bag that was actually a plant. Maybe she needed her eyes testing? But Pearl had seen the sleeping bag too. What was going on?

"Hey Matilda," called Violet. "I've just had a good idea. Remember that lesson we had with Ms Rivers on the Heart Tree?"

Matilda screwed up her eyes as she did her best

to remember. "The oldest tree on the island?" she ventured.

"That's the one. Well it's right here, in the middle of the dell."

"Don't lots of pink chinchillas live in its branches?" Matilda remembered.

"Yes," said Rosa. "Over the Heart Tree's lifetime it's absorbed lots of magic from the island. Pink chinchillas are drawn to magic and made their home there centuries ago."

"And … chinchillas moult at this time of year!" Violet smiled. "Their fur is super soft and we need something pink for the scavenger hunt. If we could find some pink chinchilla fur we could take some for the scavenger hunt and some for you to put on the heather to make it softer." She looked at Rosa. "What do you think?"

"It's a brilliant idea!" said Rosa, high-fiving her. "And on the way to the Heart Tree we can look

for more of the scavenger hunt things. Let's go!"

Matilda breathed a sigh of relief. Maybe she hadn't ruined the hunt for everyone after all!

CHAPTER FIVE

Matilda and Pearl rode at the front as she and her friends left their camp to find the Heart Tree.

"We're going to be really helpful," she whispered to Pearl. "We'll look really hard and find as many things on the list as we can while we ride. Then the others won't think I'm useless."

"You're definitely not useless," Pearl said, loyally. "You're great!"

"Thanks." Matilda stroked Pearl's neck but she was still smarting from the others' words. Did Freya and Rosa really think she was stupid, and did Ariana really think her drawings were just

scribbles? She swallowed, feeling unusually down in the dumps. She wasn't used to feeling that her friends were unhappy with her.

"Is that Valentina?" Violet said suddenly. "What is she doing? And look at that chair!"

In the middle of a circle of trees, Valentina was sitting on a comfy blue chair that was padded with silver cushions. She was shouting out instructions to the other girls in Ruby dorm, who were busy running around her.

"Valentina, I've found something pink. It's up there, at the top of that tree. It looks like a feather from a rose finch," said Isla, a petite girl with short brown hair.

"I don't want to just hear about it. Go and get it," said Valentina, bossily.

"But it's too high for me to climb."

Valentina stared up at the tree. "It is high but Golden Briar can get it down with his wind magic.

Where is he?"

"I'm here." Golden Briar was munching on a bucket of sky berries while the other unicorns were helping their girls. He wandered over. "You need my wind magic again? What for this time?"

Valentina and Golden Briar were second years. Golden Briar had found his magic last year but as he hadn't bonded with Valentina they hadn't been allowed to graduate, so had stayed at the academy.

"See that pink feather up there? Blow it down!" Valentina reached for a chocolate from the bag next to her. Her face tightened when she noticed Matilda and her dorm-mates approaching. "I mean, I wish we could use your wind magic to get the feather," she said hurriedly. "But we can't because that would be cheating. And Ruby dorm would never cheat, would we, girls?"

Isla looked bewildered. "But earlier on you said

that using Golden Briar's magic wasn't cheating because—"

"Because we aren't going to use any magic," said Valentina loudly. "What are you staring at?" she added, glaring at Matilda. "Oh, I know. A successful team."

"A big fat cheating team, more like," said Matilda crossly. "I know you were going to use Golden Briar's magic to get that feather."

"You can think what you like. You didn't see anything. And personally, I don't think having magic would make any difference to your chances, Matilda. Not unless it's super strong tidying magic. I mean, look at the state of you. Do you even own a comb? Oh, don't tell me, I expect it broke in that bird's nest you call hair. Go away and take your loser friends with you. You're not going to win the scavenger hunt. We are!"

Matilda tensed.

"Ignore her," said Violet. "She's not worth it."

"You're right." Matilda breathed out slowly. "Let's go."

"Ruby dorm can't be allowed to cheat," said Ariana angrily, as the Diamond girls rode away.

"I know, it's not fair," Violet agreed. "But what can we do? If we tell the teachers then we'll just look like snitches."

"I think we should tell," said Rosa. "Cheating's wrong. What do you think Freya? Freya, are you even listening?"

Freya was sitting on Honey's back, a faraway look in her eyes. "Yes, totally," she said, blinking. "Whatever you say."

Rosa sighed in frustration.

"I hate telling tales," said Matilda. "Let's not say anything. We'll just have to make sure that Diamond dorm wins."

"Yes, let's do that!" said Rosa, looking happier.

Matilda and Pearl

On the way to the middle of the woods, they skirted a pond and Rosa found a sparkling hag stone in the water. Then Violet spotted a green feather caught on a branch.

"We're doing really well," she said. "We've got three things and the chinchilla fur will make four."

"Wow!" Matilda exclaimed as they entered a huge clearing at the centre of the dell. "Look at that!" The ancient Heart Tree was twice the size she'd expected. Caught in a ray of sunlight, its trunk shone pure gold and its slender branches arched overhead to form the shape of a heart. But as Pearl walked closer, Matilda realised something was very wrong. The tree seemed to be covered with a furry mould and instead of a fiery red, the heart-shaped leaves were wrinkled and brown. Piles of dead leaves lay in heaps at the base of the tree.

"Is that really the Heart Tree?" asked Freya.

"It can't be," said Violet. "It's dying."

Matilda got off Pearl and went to investigate. "It is the Heart Tree," she said, picking up a crinkled heart-shaped leaf from the ground.

"What's that noise?" Ariana had followed Matilda over to the Heart Tree but now she stopped to listen.

"Look!" breathed Violet, pointing at the base

of the tree. Dozens of frightened dark eyes were peering round the trunk at the girls and unicorns.

"It's the chinchillas!" said Matilda. She and the others dismounted and approached slowly. The chinchillas huddled closer together, chittering anxiously. They were surrounded by piles of soft pink fur.

One brave chinchilla left the group and scampered towards the girls. It stood up on its hind legs and chattered at them, waving its little front legs.

"I don't understand chinchilla," Matilda said, looking round at the others in concern. "But I'm pretty sure it's asking for our help!"

CHAPTER SIX

Matilda moved closer to the chinchilla, who seemed to be trying to talk to them. He squeaked in alarm and raced back to the others. They all scattered, their squeaks becoming more high-pitched as they jumped into the Heart Tree's sagging branches, sending more leaves swirling to the ground.

"Stop," called Matilda. "We're not going to hurt you. Please come back."

"They're terrified. Whisper, can you help?" asked Ariana.

Whisper had soothing magic. It meant he could

calm animals and people whenever they were anxious or angry. Tossing his mane, he lifted a hoof and stamped it on the ground.

Crack! Blue, pink and purple sparks swirled in the air accompanied by the delicious scent of caramelised sugar. A memory tugged at Matilda's mind. She'd recently smelt that same smell. When had it been?

But her thoughts were distracted by the sight of the chinchillas. As Whisper's magic reached them, they stopped squeaking and climbed back down to the base of the tree. Looking much calmer, they scampered towards the girls, who knelt down to greet them.

The chinchillas jumped into their laps. Matilda ended up with one on each shoulder and three in her arms. Their soft pink fur tickled her chin and their eyes were dark and sparkling. They had large round ears and they made a soft chittering sound.

"What is it?" she whispered, knowing they were trying to tell her something. "What's been happening here?"

"I bet it's something to do with the Heart Tree," said Rosa, looking up from her own armfuls of chinchillas. "I wonder why it's dying?"

"Hey, why are you all wearing chinchillas?" called a voice.

It was Miki and Himmat from Topaz dorm. Matilda smiled at them; she liked both of the boys.

"Is pink fur the new fashion?" said Himmat, laughing loudly.

"Shh, don't scare the chinchillas. Something's upset them," said Violet.

Miki and Himmat immediately stopped fooling around and looked concerned. "What do you

mean?" Himmat asked, lowering his voice.

Rosa explained what they had found. Himmat investigated the tree while Miki, who was brilliant with animals, picked up a chinchilla from the ground. He stroked it gently, starting behind its ears, then along its back and tail. The chinchilla relaxed into Miki's arms. Miki frowned. "Something's definitely wrong. Look how patchy its fur is in places. I know chinchillas moult at this time of year but their coats should always look glossy and healthy. Himmat, can you pick me some leaves from those small white flowers? Yes, those ones," he added as Himmat pointed to a shady area dotted with tiny white star shapes.

"Everyone, try feeding the chinchillas these leaves," Miki

urged as Himmat handed him a leaf and he offered it to his chinchilla. "They're good for chinchillas, they've got lots of the vitamins they need and they help calm them down."

The chinchillas munched on the leaves, staring at the children with huge eyes as if they were waiting for them to do something.

Miki pushed his long black fringe out of his eyes. "I don't understand it. Whatever it is that's upsetting the chinchillas, it must be very serious for their coats to be affected."

"I think it's got to be something to do with the tree," said Violet.

"I vote we find Ms Rivers and tell her about it," said Ariana.

"I agree," said Rosa, "but let's finish the scavenger hunt first and then tell her. A couple more hours won't make any difference. It would be so annoying to let Valentina win, especially

since it sounds like she's cheating." Rosa put the chinchilla she was cuddling down at the base of the Heart Tree. Then she pulled a ball of pink fur from her top. "This will do for the scavenger hunt. Come on, let's get going. We'll sort out the chinchillas and collect some fur for Matilda to sleep on later."

"We'd better get going too," said Miki. He placed his chinchilla down and plucked some fur from the ground. "You're right, a few more hours won't matter. Hopefully Ms Rivers will be able to sort it out. She knows lots about animals."

Everyone jumped back on their unicorns, but Matilda hesitated.

"Come on, Matilda," said Pearl nudging her. But Matilda was longing to draw the Heart Tree.

"Just give me a few minutes," she begged, pulling her sketchbook out. "I'll catch you up in a sec!" she called to the others, who had started

riding away. "Don't wait!" She didn't want to stop them from finding the things they needed.

"OK," Rosa called back. "Don't be long!"

Silence fell and Matilda started to draw. The tree looked so sad with its fallen leaves but it was also still strangely beautiful. What had happened to it? Her fingers flew across the page. The chinchillas scampered around her feet but then suddenly they froze, their large ears swivelling. Matilda listened and then she heard it too – the sound of hoof beats. At once, the chinchillas fled. Scrambling over each other, they raced into the surrounding bushes.

"Matilda," said Pearl breathlessly. "Look!"

Matilda followed Pearl's gaze and inhaled sharply. A figure cloaked in black was cantering towards the clearing, riding a golden-maned unicorn. The unicorn's hoof beats grew louder as it carried the hooded figure closer. Icy fingers

swept down Matilda's spine – was this the person responsible for the Heart Tree dying and the chinchillas' fear?

She vaulted on to Pearl's back but it was too late for them to escape. She gripped Pearl's mane. "What are we going to do now?" she whispered.

CHAPTER SEVEN

Pearl cantered towards a bright orange bush at the edge of the clearing. Its twisted leaves looked like a roaring fire. "It's too small to hide us both!" cried Matilda. "We need something bigger!"

Sparks shot up in front of them and a smell of burnt sugar filled the air. Matilda squeaked in surprise and Pearl skidded to a halt as the bush suddenly doubled in size.

"What just happened?" gasped Matilda.

"It's my magic!" said Pearl. "Those sparks came from my hooves. I was wishing the bush was bigger and suddenly it was!" She dashed behind it. "I

must have glamour magic – it means I can create illusions for a short time. My aunt has it too, it's awesome."

"Glamour magic! Oh, wow!" That explained all the strange things Matilda had seen recently – the wings, the sleeping bag. But she didn't have time to think any more about it. "Shh!" she hissed as she peered round the bush and saw the hooded figure cantering into the clearing.

"Um, Matilda, I don't know how long I can hold the glamour for," Pearl whispered, her breath tickling Matilda's ear. "My aunt always told me it's hard to control a glamour at first. Stay as still as you can, that should make it easier for me."

Matilda nodded, pressing a finger to her lips. Her heart pounded loudly as she watched the person leap from their unicorn in a swirl of black cloth. Matilda tried to see their face but the hood hid it well.

Furtively, the figure glanced around and then walked over to the Heart Tree. They took out a round glass bottle from a bag tied at their waist and set it at the foot of the Heart Tree. Then they drew something else from under their cloak. It flashed in the sunlight. Matilda almost gasped out loud. A knife! The figure made a long, deep cut in the tree's trunk. Tossing the knife on the ground, the figure lifted the bottle to the cut and caught the deep-red sap that oozed from the trunk.

Matilda could hardly bear to watch as the magical sap drained into the bottle. The tree's branches drooped even further as their life force drained away, leaving just a few stray droplets glittering on the bark. If only she could get a glimpse of the figure. She leaned forward…

"Matilda!" Pearl whispered in alarm. "Don't move! The glamour's fading!"

Matilda's breath caught in her throat as the pretend bush hiding them started to tremble and dissolve.

"Make another one!" hissed Matilda.

"I can't," Pearl panted. "My magic's not strong enough yet."

"Then gallop!" screamed Matilda, vaulting on to Pearl as the figure glanced round. Pearl raced into the woods, heading for the track that led back to the campsite. Matilda dared to look back, expecting to see the dark figure and the unicorn with the golden mane chasing after them, but to her astonishment she saw that the chinchillas had come charging out from the bushes and had leapt at the person's cloak, hanging on to it with tiny claws and running up the sleeves.

"No! Get off, you little pests!" It was a woman's voice but Matilda didn't stop to hear any more. Leaning forward, she urged Pearl through the

dense trees until they broke out on to the track. Matilda realised that Pearl was not galloping as fast as normal – doing magic had clearly tired her out.

"Keep going," Matilda urged her. "Come on, Pearl!" She stroked Pearl's neck, hoping her unicorn would feel her love. Finding an extra surge of energy, Pearl raced along the track,

leaving the sinister figure behind.

"Look! There's everyone, up ahead." Matilda sat back and Pearl slowed down. "We're safe now. I don't think they followed us. Well done, Pearl. You did brilliantly."

"So did you. You were really brave," panted Pearl. "Thanks for not panicking."

"It's my fault we nearly got caught. If only I hadn't moved, then you would have held the glamour and that horrible person would never have seen us."

"That's not true," said Pearl. "It's much easier to hold a glamour if you keep still but I was already losing that one. It was my fault for not having better control of my magic yet."

"No. I'm to blame, not you," said Matilda. "I promise to listen more carefully in future." Matilda hugged Pearl's neck. "Thanks for being the most brilliant unicorn ever."

Matilda and Pearl

"And thanks for being the best friend a unicorn could have," said Pearl. She tossed her head. "Now let's go and tell the others what we saw!"

CHAPTER EIGHT

Rosa was ticking items off their scavenger hunt list while the other Diamond dorm girls held out their finds. Matilda and Pearl cantered into the centre of the group.

"Oh, there you are, Matilda. We thought we were going to have to come back and get you. We've done really well – Freya found a six-petal daisy so now all we need is an orange leaf. If we find one quickly, we could win!" Rosa finished triumphantly.

"Are you OK?" Violet asked, seeing Matilda's pale face.

"There was a cloaked figure. It chased us!" Matilda blurted out.

The others frowned. "Really?" said Rosa doubtfully.

"Is this one of your jokes, Matilda?" asked Ariana. "Because if it is, it's not very funny."

"Yes, we haven't really got time to mess around now," said Freya.

"Not if we want to get back before Valentina's team," added Violet.

"I'm not making it up!" exclaimed Matilda. "It's true!" She told them everything that had just happened. She didn't leave anything out, even telling them the part when she'd not remembered to stay still and caused Pearl's glamour to collapse. "The chinchillas were brilliant," she added. "They stopped the person from chasing us."

Ariana frowned. "You don't sound like you're

teasing," she said, doubtfully.

"I'm not!" said Matilda in frustration. Why wouldn't her friends believe her?

"Matilda is telling the truth," said Pearl, backing her up.

"She must be!" spluttered Freya. "Look everyone!" She pointed at Matilda's hair. "Matilda's got a streak of pink and yellow in her hair. She's bonded with Pearl!"

Matilda tipped her head forward and stared in surprise at the pink and yellow lock of hair, the exact same shade as Pearl's mane. Happiness rushed through her. Now the others would have to believe her!

"Oh, wow!" said Rosa. "Glamour magic is so cool and useful, too."

"Hang on," said Ariana anxiously. "If the story's true, shouldn't we be getting out of here? I can't imagine the chinchillas will be able to stop

the person for long."

"Shh!" said Freya, suddenly holding up her hand. "Can anyone hear that?"

Immediately, everyone stopped talking and listened.

"Hoof beats. Oh no! They did follow us!" Pearl's ears flickered anxiously. "Quick everyone, gallop!"

"Too late!" The golden-maned unicorn charged out from the trees, the hooded figure steering it straight towards the girls. Her voice, muffled by the cloak, was harsh and bitter. "This time I'll put an end to your medalling ways."

Her unicorn stopped in a shower of sparks. Lifting its hoof, it stamped on the ground. The earth started to move, spiralling upwards into a mini tornado of glittering red and yellow sparkles. The tornado buzzed as it spun towards

the girls. Then, suddenly, it broke apart.

"Hex hornets!" shrieked Matilda, as the huge, angry insects flew at the girls and the unicorns. They all scattered in alarm. Hex hornets would chase people for hours and gave terrible stings.

The hex hornets reached Ariana and Whisper first. Whisper reared up in a panic and Ariana shrieked and tumbled off his back. As always, the island's magic formed a pink bubble around

her, cushioning her fall so she wasn't hurt. But as the bubble carried Ariana safely to the ground, the hex hornets encircled Whisper, making it impossible for her to reach him.

The figure cackled with laughter. "Time for a little binding spell, next, I think!" They began to draw something from their cloak as clouds of hex hornets buzzed towards the other girls. Pearl whinnied and turned to bolt away.

"Wait!" cried Matilda, looking back and seeing the others all being surrounded. "We can't leave them! Do something, Pearl. Turn into a tiger or something."

"I can't," said Pearl, stopping. "I'm too tired for my magic to work."

"You can do it!" said Matilda, leaping off Pearl's back and seeing the figure riding towards Ariana with a hand outstretched. "You're totally brilliant at everything!"

"OK, I'll try." Pearl slammed her hoof on the ground. Sparks spluttered in the air and dissolved. The cloaked figure looked round and laughed scornfully.

"Pathetic! You haven't got any magic that can hurt me."

"You're the pathetic one, harming innocent creatures!" screamed Matilda. "Try again, Pearl. You can do this. I know you can!"

Matilda and Pearl

Pearl took a deep breath and stamped so hard the ground shook. A fountain of pink sparks shot up into the air and suddenly Pearl vanished. In her place stood a giant orange-and-black striped tiger with legs as thick as tree trunks. Matilda heard her dorm-mates gasp and saw their astonished faces. The tiger threw back its head and roared furiously, showing its enormous teeth.

"Shape-shifting magic!" the figure said in horror. "Go!" she screamed to her unicorn. It bolted through the trees, kicking up leaves and twigs as it raced away with Pearl, the tiger, chasing behind.

CHAPTER NINE

Matilda watched in delight as Pearl, disguised as a tiger, roared and sprinted after the panicked unicorn. She had no idea how Pearl was finding the strength to use her magic when she was already so tired. The cloaked figure and her unicorn crashed through the trees and disappeared from sight.

"Pearl," yelled Matilda. "You can stop now. She's gone!"

As Pearl slowed and turned back, her stripes faded and her body changed from a stocky tiger with huge paws back to a slender unicorn. Matilda realised the hornets had disappeared along with

the cloaked person. A thought flashed across her mind: *Perhaps they have glamor magic too.*

Pearl walked back to Matilda, her sides heaving.

"That was incredible!" gasped Rosa.

"Wasn't it?" Matilda was glowing. "You were so brave, Pearl. I don't know how you did that when you were so tired."

"I did it because you believed in me. You gave me the confidence to find more energy when I thought I was exhausted." Pearl pushed her head into Matilda's arms. Matilda hugged her tightly. "It was lucky the person thought I was a shape-shifter," Pearl went on. "If she'd realised it was just a glamour she'd have known I couldn't really hurt her. My tiger teeth might have looked sharp but they couldn't do any real damage."

"Which makes you even braver for chasing her away," said Matilda.

"I'm really tired now," panted Pearl.

"We need sky berries," said Freya. "They'll help Pearl get her energy back."

"But we left them all by the tents," said Violet in dismay. "We left all the heavy stuff there with the rucksacks and tents – remember?"

"It's OK, I've got some," said Ariana. She opened up the small knapsack she'd been carrying. "I brought an emergency supply with me just in case." She handed a pile of sky berries to Matilda who fed Pearl handfuls of them until her breathing slowed down and she started to look better.

"Thank you," Matilda said gratefully, giving the empty bag back to Ariana. "I'm really glad you're always prepared for anything."

"That's OK, thank you for saving me," Ariana replied. They

smiled at each other. "I'm sorry I said your drawings were scribbles earlier," Ariana went on quickly. "I didn't mean it at all, your drawings are brilliant. I was just cross about you forgetting your sleeping bag."

"I'm not surprised, it was stupid of me," Matilda admitted. "I should have read the list you gave me and made sure I had everything before we left." She looked round at her friends. "I promise I'll try and be more organised and less distracted by drawing from now on." She bit her bottom lip. "We're probably going to lose the competition because of me. If I hadn't stopped to sketch the Heart Tree we'd have been back by now."

"But then we wouldn't have found out about the person harming the Heart Tree," said Rosa. "That's far more important than any competition. We need to get back and tell Ms Rivers straight away."

"Even though we still haven't got everything for the scavenger hunt?" said Matilda. "You said we still needed an orange leaf, didn't you?"

"The safety of Unicorn Island is far more important than winning a scavenger hunt!" said Rosa. "I know I like to win but the island comes first."

"Definitely. It's more important than anything. I think we should find Ms Rivers as quickly as we can," said Freya, nodding.

"OK." Matilda put her hand on Pearl's mane to vault on to her back.

"Matilda, what's that orange thing in your hair?" Pearl said suddenly.

"You mean the streak of hair that shows we've bonded?' said Matilda. "It's not orange, is it? Your mane is yellow and pink."

"I know that, silly! No – I mean, what's this? Look!" Pearl pulled a small orange leaf from

Matilda's hair with her teeth.

"It must be from the bush when we were hiding behind it!" exclaimed Matilda.

Rosa shrieked in delight. "Matilda! You must have hidden behind a flame bush! That's the last thing we need for the scavenger hunt!"

"We can still win!" said Ariana.

"If we get back before anyone else," said Freya.

"What are we waiting for?" Matilda cried, excitement buzzing through her. "Let's go!"

They galloped flat out, all the way back to the teacher's campsite. Matilda didn't let herself get distracted by anything on the way back. There was no way she was going to be responsible for Diamond dorm not winning now!

As Pearl swept past the white tree at the entrance to the woods, Matilda saw the boys from Topaz dorm standing around Ms Rivers, talking

earnestly. They must have got back first. Her heart sank.

Rosa and Crystal halted beside Ms Rivers. "Did you beat us?" Rosa demanded breathlessly, looking at Miki and Himmat.

"No," said Miki. "We didn't read the list properly and we forgot we needed a hag stone. We went back to the Heart Tree to get an orange leaf because Himmat remembered there was a flame bush there but when we got there, we found that in the grass by the tree!"

He pointed to an object in Ms Rivers' hands. Matilda's eyes widened as she saw that it was a silver knife – the very same knife she had seen the cloaked figure using on the Heart Tree.

"I don't know what it was doing by the Heart Tree," Ms Rivers said. "But I've sent a message to Ms Nettles and she's on her way here. The boys say the tree seems to be dying and—"

88

Matilda and Pearl

"I know what's happening!" Matilda burst out.

For once, Ms Rivers didn't tell her off for interrupting. "What do you mean, Matilda?" she demanded.

The story tumbled out of Matilda's mouth. Everything she had seen: the cloaked figure with the knife in the clearing, the way she had chased Matilda and Pearl. The others chipped in too when it came to describing how she had found them and attacked them and how Pearl had scared her off.

Ms Nettles and Ms Bramble arrived when they were halfway through and they had to say it all over again.

All three teachers were looking very grave by the time the girls had finished.

"This person must be draining magic away from the Heart Tree," said Ms Nettles. "The red liquid Matilda saw is its magical life force.

The person who did this is clearly extremely dangerous. Did you see her face, girls? Could you describe her?"

"No, she was covered by a cloak and a hood and her voice was quite muffled," said Rosa.

"Can I see the knife please?" said Ms Bramble. Ms Rivers passed it to her.

Ms Bramble gasped. "But this is my knife!" She turned the silver knife over in her hands as she examined it. "I locked it in the store cupboard

this morning after I'd been out with Ms Willow fixing the quiverleaf tree. I have no idea how it got here."

"We will have to investigate," said Ms Nettles grimly.

"Do you think it's the same person who stopped the waterfall?" said Rosa curiously.

"We will not waste time guessing without any evidence," said Ms Nettles. "The two incidents may be linked or they may be totally unrelated. For now, our priority has to be saving the Heart Tree. Ms Bramble, can you do anything for it?"

"I think so. I could also arrange for the gardeners to watch over it to prevent a further attack, if you'd like me to? They will be able to protect the chinchillas too."

"That sounds like a very good idea," said Ms Nettles. She sneezed loudly. "Excuse me everyone, my hay fever is playing up. I will return to school but I will ask all available teachers to patrol Dingleberry Dell to ensure everyone's safety during the night. We can talk more in the morning when the camping trip is over."

In the distance there was the sound of

galloping hooves. Matilda tensed. Had the hooded figure returned? But as the hooves grew louder, she saw that it was a group of students riding towards them. The lead unicorn had a long golden mane and flowing tail and its rider, Valentina, punched the air with a fist as she passed the white tree.

"We're back! I won! I mean – Ruby dorm won!" she hastily corrected herself.

She jumped from Golden Briar's back and then noticed everyone standing there. "What!" she spluttered. "How come Topaz and Diamond dorm finished before us? Did you cheat? I bet you did," she said accusingly to Matilda.

Matilda held Valentina's eye. "Why ever would you think that?" she asked sweetly. "Diamond dorm are definitely not cheats."

"No, we are not!" chorused her friends.

"Unlike other people around here," muttered

Rosa, nudging Matilda.

Valentina glared at her.

"Let me check you have everything on the list, Diamond dorm," said Ms Rivers. Rosa handed her the bag with everything in it. The teacher checked the contents while Valentina folded her arms and muttered to her dorm-mates.

"Well, I'm happy to declare that Diamond dorm is indeed the winner!" Ms Rivers said.

"Gah!" Valentina exclaimed, her face now as sour as a lemon. She stomped away, leaving her dorm-mates to shyly congratulate Matilda and her friends.

"Well done, girls," Ms Rivers said to Diamond dorm.

Miki sighed. "We'd have won if we'd not forgotten the hag stone."

"You should always read lists very carefully, Miki," said Matilda in a mock-strict voice.

Ariana squealed in delight. "Now that's something I never thought I'd hear you say, Matilda!"

Matilda grinned. "Well, I guess I've learnt stuff today." She looked round at all her friends. "And not just that I need to be a bit more organised in future. I've learnt how amazing my unicorn is, how brilliant all my friends are and how much I love having fun with them all!"

Ms Rivers' strict face softened for once. "Then I'd advise you to go and carry on having fun," she said. "You all definitely deserve it. Let me get your prize for winning." She fetched two bags of enormous pink and white marshmallows and gave them to Matilda.

"Yum!" said Freya.

Matilda handed one bag to Miki. "Here," she said. "I think Topaz dorm should have this."

He fist-bumped her. "Cool, thanks!"

"Right off you go back to your campsites," said Ms Rivers. "Oh, and if anyone has forgotten anything, now is the time to say so. I have spares of most things. Matilda, is there something you're missing, maybe?"

"Um, my sleeping bag," said Matilda sheepishly.

"What? You mean this one?" said Ms Rivers, going to her tent and pulling out a purple sleeping bag.

Matilda gaped. "How did you know?"

"I did a quick check of the stables before we left," said Ms Rivers, some of her usual strictness creeping back into her expression. "I

didn't tell you earlier because I thought that if it slowed your team down then it might teach you a valuable lesson."

"It did," said Matilda. "And I won't forget it." She grinned at Ms Rivers as she took the sleeping bag. "Thank you, Miss."

"Now go on! Shoo!" said Ms Rivers, flapping her hands at them.

It wasn't long before the Diamond dorm girls and their unicorns were happily settled in their camp. The unicorns munched on sky berries while the girls busied themselves getting the camp organised and setting up a roaring campfire. Matilda wanted to make some sketches so that she could paint the scene later but she resisted and put her sketchbook inside her sleeping bag, where she wouldn't be tempted by it. She mucked in with everyone

else, doing her fair share of the chores. It wasn't long before everything was neat and tidy. Ariana let out a contented sigh. "Shall we toast the marshmallows now?"

"Yes, let's!" said Matilda, going to get the long toasting forks that Ariana had packed.

They sat round the campfire, listening to the hiss of the flames as the marshmallows turned soft and gooey.

"I love camping," said Violet happily.

"Me too," said Rosa.

"This is quite fun," said Freya. "It's actually nice having a night off from my invention. What?! Where's the fire gone?" she exclaimed as she found herself toasting her marshmallow over an icy water fountain.

"Pearl!" Matilda giggled as she looked round to see that her unicorn had crept up behind them.

"Busted!" Pearl said. She stamped her hoof and

the water fountain turned back into flickering red and gold flames.

"Your magic's so cool!" said Violet.

"How about this?" said Pearl. Looking at Ariana's tent, she stamped her hoof. It turned into a miniature castle with turrets, flags and a drawbridge.

"Oh, that's so pretty. I wish I could sleep in that tonight!" said Ariana.

"I don't think I can hold the glamour for a whole night!" As Pearl spoke the castle became a tent with a turret perched at one end. There were shouts of laughter as it slowly faded to reveal the normal tent.

Matilda blew on a toasted marshmallow then popped it into her mouth. As the chewy sweet dissolved on her tongue she felt incredibly happy. She loved studying at Unicorn Academy. She'd made a great bunch of friends and Pearl was the

very best unicorn.

"I meant what I said earlier," she told her friends as she threaded another marshmallow on to her toasting fork. "From now on, I'm going to try and be more organised. And I'm going to stop joking around so much. It was horrid when you didn't believe me about the hooded figure."

"Well, don't change too much," said Rosa, giving Matilda a hug. "We like you the way you are."

"Yes, don't get too sensible," said Ariana.

Matilda grinned. "I don't think there's much chance of that!"

"Group hug," said Violet. "Come on, Freya. That means you too!"

Freya rolled her eyes. "Really?" she grumbled, but she got up to join in the group hug. "The others are right. You're not that bad," she added quietly to Matilda.

"Aw, thanks," said Matilda, knocking her cheek against Freya's.

"Who wants a hot chocolate?" asked Violet, breaking away. "We can float some of the marshmallows on top."

As everyone busied themselves making hot chocolate and toasting more marshmallows, Pearl nudged Matilda. "The others are right, don't change too much, Matilda. I love you the way you are. You're my perfect partner."

"And you're mine," Matilda wrapped her arms around Pearl's neck and hugged her tightly. "I'm so lucky to have you!"

She looked up and saw a huge sparkly red heart hanging in the sky. She rubbed her eyes and when she looked again she saw it was just the moon.

"Pearl!" she giggled.

Pearl blinked at her, her dark eyes sparkling like the stars overhead. "Friends forever?" she said.

"Forever!" Matilda declared.

"Matilda, where are you?" called Violet. "The hot chocolate's ready."

"Coming!" Matilda kissed Pearl and, with her heart brimming with happiness, she ran to join her friends.

PRINCESS of PETS

Look out for a BRILLIANT new Nosy Crow series from the author of The Rescue Princesses!

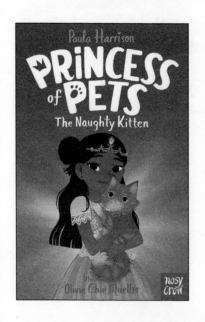

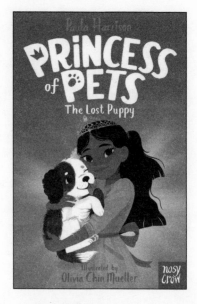

Animal adventures, friendship and a royal family!

FUNNY FICTION
FROM NOSY CROW

Another MAGICAL series from Nosy Crow!

SNOW SISTERS

LOOK OUT FOR
THE JASMINE GREEN SERIES!